Freaky Francie

by Sibyl Hancock

illustrated by Leonard Shortall

Prentice-Hall, Inc., Englewood Cliffs, N.J.

Library of Congress Cataloging in Publication Data
Hancock, Sibyl.
Freaky Francie.
SUMMARY: Beth's babysitter uses extrasensory
perception to help locate a pin Beth has lost.
[1. Extrasensory perception—Fiction. 2. Babysit-
ters—Fiction] I. Shortall, Leonard. II. Title
PZ7.H1916Fr   [Fic]   79-15226
ISBN 0-13-330563-5

For Ellen Goins, with love

Francie looked at the bookcase.
She was hunting for a good mystery.
Since babysitting wasn't her favorite pastime,
she might as well read.
Francie found a book and started reading.
The story was exciting.
A door slammed, and Beth and Alan ran into
the room.

"Francie! Something awful has happened!"
cried Beth. "We have lost the pearl pin my mom
wears on her dresses!"

"Fiddlesticks!" Francie said. "Why did this have to happen while I'm minding you? Your mom won't be pleased."

"I told Beth that Freaky Francie would help," said Alan. He rolled his eyes and made a silly face.

"Don't call me freaky!" Francie yelled. "Just because I have E.S.P. doesn't make me freaky. Besides, when you make that silly face you look freaky yourself."

"What is E.S.P.?" Beth asked.

"Extra sensory perception," Francie answered. "I'm extra good at finding lost things."

"See!" Alan said. "Freaky!"

Francie ignored him. "This does sound like a good case. Be right with you."

Francie opened her purse. She pulled out her magnifying glass. No real detective would ever be caught without one.

"All right, where is the scene of the crime?" Francie asked.

"It isn't a crime!" said Beth as she began sniffling.

"In other words, where do you think you lost the pin?" questioned Francie.

"In my playhouse," Beth said. "We were playing dress-up."

"I can see that," Francie said. "Let's go to the playhouse and have a look around."

It was a large playhouse in Beth's backyard.

Francie moved around carefully. She examined the dolls, the dishes and the old furniture. Beth had more dolls than anyone Francie had ever known.

"What does the pin look like?" Francie asked.

"It has pearls on it and is shaped like a heart," Beth said. "Daddy gave it to Mom when they first met."

"Pink pumpkins!" Alan whistled. "That old pin must be an antique!"

Beth again started to cry.

"Stop that sniffling," Francie said. "We have work to do. First things first. Let's search the playhouse."

"We have already done that," Alan said.

"So do it again," Francie said.

Alan grinned and yanked Francie's hair.

"Stop pulling my hair!" she said. "Get busy
hunting for that pin!"

They looked—and looked—and looked, but
found no pearl pin.

"The pin is lost," Francie said.

"We told you that," Alan answered. "You're
some detective!"

"Wait!" Francie yelled. "I'm getting a *feeling.*"
She shut her eyes tight and stood very still.
Then she snapped her fingers.

"BLACK!" she yelled. "The pin has been around something black! What around here is black?"

"A blackboard," Alan said. "A rubber tire? A black cat?"

"It has to make sense," Francie told him.

Beth thought and thought. "Puddles, my dog. He's black."

"Aha!" Francie said. "Does he bury bones?"

"Yes," Beth said.

"Then we will dig in your backyard," Francie said.

They dug—and dug—and dug.

They found bones, a quarter and a rusty nail.

But no pearl pin.

Alan kept the quarter. "Finders keepers," he said.

Francie rubbed her hands. They hurt after doing all that digging. She just had to find the pin!

"Now what?" Beth asked.

"I'll have to think," Francie said.

Then it happened.

"Wait!" Francie yelled. "I'm getting another *feeling!*"

She shut her eyes tight and stood very still.

Then she snapped her fingers.

"GREEN!" she yelled. "The pin has something to do with green!"

"Grass is green," Alan said.

"Now that took some real thought," Francie said. "Not many people know grass is green."

Alan looked cross-eyed. "At least I'm not freaky!"

"You're a pain in the neck," Francie said. "And don't call me freaky!" Sometimes she got awfully tired of Alan.

"How about green soda pop bottles? Or green lizards?" Beth asked.

"Hmm," Francie said. "Maybe it is grass. Did you kids walk anywhere other than this yard?"

"Sure," Beth said. "We went to Alan's house."

"Why didn't you say so?" Francie said. "The pin is in the grass somewhere by the sidewalk."

"Pink pumpkins! You mean we have to look through all that grass?" Alan cried. He ran his hand through his hair until it stood up in points.

"That's right!" Francie said. She wasn't about
to give up.

And so they looked—and looked—and looked.
They found some bottle caps, a paper clip, and
a piece of dirty string.

But no pearl pin.

"Now that we are at my house," Alan said, "let's eat something. How about an apple?" Alan was always hungry.

Francie figured even detectives had to rest. Besides, she never turned down apples.

Francie was almost finished with her apple when it happened again.

"Wait!" she yelled. "Another *feeling!*"
She shut her eyes tight and stood very still.
Then she snapped her fingers.
  "RED!" she yelled. "The pin is around some-
thing red."

"Lipstick is red," Beth said. "And balloons.
And fire trucks. And cherries. And..."

"Shh!" Francie said. "Slow down and think."
"My bedroom carpet is red," Alan said.
"What are we waiting for!" Francie cried.

They looked all over the carpet. And since
Alan's room was pretty messy, it wasn't easy.

"How about under the bed?" Beth asked.

"Good idea," Francie said.

"Are there any spiders under there?" Beth asked. "I'm scared of spiders."

"Boo!" Alan yelled. And Beth almost started crying again.

"Don't be such a fraidy cat," Francie said.

They all poked their heads under the bed. But there was nothing there except some dust.

Alan's mother walked into the room. "What is going on?" she asked.

Whack!

Whack!

Whack!

Three heads bumped the bed.

"Ouch!" Alan said, rubbing his head. "We are just looking for something."

"Oh," his mother said. She went back to her ironing.

"Could there by anything else red?" Francie asked.

"Hey!" Alan yelled. "That fuzzy old robe of Pop's I had on is red! That's why I came home. It was too hot to wear. I wanted to get Pop's old hat."

31

Francie sighed. "Why didn't you say so? Does the robe have pockets?"

"Big ones," Alan said.

"Well, where is it?" Francie asked.

Alan looked on his closet floor. It wasn't there.

"Mom," he called, "where is that old red robe?"

"I gave it to the junk man a few minutes ago,"
she said.

"Oh no!" Alan cried.

And Beth started sniffling again.

"The junk man is probably still around here," Francie said. "Let's find him. I'll bet that pin fell into one of those robe pockets!"

They found the junk man on the next street.

"Where is the red robe?" Francie asked him.

"Underneath the junk somewhere," he said. "You're free to look."

"You mean we've got to look through all that?"
Alan cried.

"That's right," Francie said.

They dug through pots and pans, old tires, and
just plain junk. Francie got a streak of dirt on her
face. But she wouldn't let a little dirt bother her.

"I found it!" Beth yelled.

Sure enough. There was the old red robe. But
Alan could find no pin in the pockets.

"Do you want the robe?" the junk man asked.

"Want it!" Alan said. "I hope I never see it
again!"

But he thanked the junk man anyway.
"I'm tired! I give up! I quit!" Alan said.
And Beth started crying.
"Never give up," Francie said. "Great detectives never quit. And, Beth, for goodness sake stop that sniffling. We will go back to the scene of the crime."

"It was not a crime!" Beth wailed.

"Never fear," Francie said. "I'll find that pin yet!"

"Freaky!" Alan mumbled.

Beth sniffled all the way back to the playhouse.

Alan talked to himself.

And Francie thought about black and green and red.

"Now everyone hush," Francie told them.

Alan grumbled. Beth and he sat on the floor and hushed.

Francie was beginning to worry. She had to find that pin, or her reputation would be ruined.

She stood very still.
Her skin felt all prickly and shivery.
She had the strongest *feeling* ever.
She walked over to two flowerpots sitting on a windowsill. One of the flowerpots had a geranium in it. The smaller one was empty. She put her hand inside the empty flowerpot.

Francie picked up a spoon. She began to dig around the geranium.

Clink!

The spoon scraped something.

Francie pulled out a very dirty, pearly pin.

"You found it!" Beth shouted.

"How did you know?" Alan asked.

"Simple," Francie said.

"The dirt in the flowerpot is *black*.

The leaves are *green*.

And the geranium is *red*.

And besides, I noticed that the dirt in the empty flowerpot is still very damp. That meant someone had just been working with it. I knew it was Beth's geranium. So I added up the clues."

"Pink pumpkins!" Alan said. "Francie! You're
not freaky. You're fantastic!"

Francie smiled a secret smile. She really didn't mind being called freaky. If she weren't a little freaky, she wouldn't know that back at home her mom had something good frying in the skillet.

Something crispy and golden brown. Something that had a wishbone and two drumsticks.

How did she know?

Francie just had a *feeling*.

E
H

Hancock, Sibyl

Freaky Francie

DATE			

© THE BAKER & TAYLOR CO.